Karen's Mermaid

**Look for these
and other books about Karen
in the
Baby-sitters Little Sister series**

Little Sister

Karen's Mermaid
Ann M. Martin

Illustrations by Susan Tang

A
LITTLE APPLE
PAPERBACK

SCHOLASTIC INC.
New York Toronto London Auckland Sydney

For the Secret Santas:
Cary, Constance, and Camy

ISBN 0-590-48299-8

12 11 10 9   4 5 6 7 8 9/0

Printed in the U.S.A.   40

First Scholastic printing, August 1994

August

"Sand and crabs and starfish and sea-shells. That is what we will see at the beach, Andrew," I said to my little brother. (He is four going on five.)

"Will we see palm trees?" he wanted to know.

"Not in New Jersey. I think we will just see pine trees and regular trees."

"Darn," said Andrew. "I wanted to climb a palm tree and pick a coconut. I wanted to crack it open and eat it."

"Andrew, you do not even like coconut," I said.

"Yes, I do!"

"No, you do not!"

"Kids!" called Mommy. "Find something to do besides argue."

It was August. Andrew and I were enjoying our summer vacation. Mommy was not. She said it was high time we went back to school. Well, we would be going back to school in a few weeks. But in between we were going to do something really fun. We were going to go to Sea City, a beach in New Jersey, for two whole weeks. Mommy and Andrew and Seth and I. (Seth is my stepfather.)

Andrew and I are part of two families— Mommy's family and Daddy's family. (Our parents are divorced.) We go back and forth between our families, a month here, a month there. Last month, in July, we lived at Daddy's house. Now we were at Mommy's house. And in a day or two we would leave for Sea City. We were excited.

Guess what. We would have friends in Sea City. Another family from Stoneybrook (that is the Connecticut town we live in) was going to rent a house there at the same time we were going to rent a house. The family was the Pikes. They have *eight* children. I do not know the Pikes *very* well, because they do not go to my school. But I know them a little. One of the Pikes, Margo, is seven years old. Just my age. I had played with Margo a few times that summer. I had decided something about her. Margo was a bossy bragger. But I could live with that.

You know what? Some people have told *me* that *I* am a bossy bragger. I am not sure this is true. One of the people who told me that was Margo. She said, "Karen Brewer, you are a bossy bragger!"

I replied, "It takes one to know one."

I do know I have a big mouth. There is no question about that. Everybody, and I mean everybody, always has to remind me not to talk so much or so loudly. They say,

"Indoor voice, Karen." I try to remember, but sometimes it is hard.

"Karen?" asked Andrew. (We had moved outside, in case we argued again. That way Mommy would not hear us.) "What else will we see in Sea City?"

"Hmm. I do not know *exactly*," I replied. I have not been to Sea City before. Margo has, though. Lots of times. Her family goes almost every summer. In fact, that was one of the things Margo had been bragging about. She thought she knew everything about Sea City. She had been saying to me, "Karen, in Sea City you can do this," or, "In Sea City we always go to . . ."

"You really do not know?" Andrew asked me.

"Well, I know what our house will look like," I said. "Seth showed me a picture of it. It is little, but it looks cozy. It is one story high, so all the rooms are on the first floor, even the bedrooms. And it has a big porch and it is right on the beach. We can stand

4

on the porch and look at the ocean. What do you think of that?"

"Cool," said Andrew. "Karen? Is there a boardwalk in Sea City?"

"I am not sure. But I know somebody who will know."

"Margo Pike?" said Andrew.

"No," I replied crossly. "Kristy. Kristy will know. She has been to Sea City. I am going to call her right now."

Kristy

Kristy is my big stepsister. Her whole name is Kristin Amanda Thomas, and she is thirteen years old. Kristy lives with Daddy's family.

I think I better tell you how I got my two families. I did not always have two families. At first I had just one — Mommy, Daddy, Andrew, me. That was a long time ago, when I was a little kid. But Mommy and Daddy were not happy together. Finally they decided they did not love each other anymore. They loved Andrew and me very much, but not each other. So they decided to divorce. After the divorce, Daddy stayed in the big house we had lived in. (It is the house he grew up in.) Mommy moved to a little house. Both of the houses are here in Stoneybrook. Later they got married again, but not to each other. Mommy married Seth. (That is how he became my stepfather.) And Daddy married Elizabeth. (Now she is my stepmother.) So Andrew and I have two families, one at the little house and one at the big house.

At the little house are Mommy, Seth, Andrew, me, Rocky, Midgie, Emily Junior, and Bob. Rocky and Midgie are Seth's cat and dog. Emily Junior is my pet rat. Bob is Andrew's hermit crab.

You will not believe who lives at the big house. It is amazing. Daddy, Elizabeth, Kristy, Charlie, Sam, David Michael, Emily Michelle, Nannie, Andrew, me, Shannon, Boo-Boo, Goldfishie, Crystal Light, Emily Junior, and Bob. (Emily Junior and Bob go back and forth when Andrew and I do.)

Are you confused? Don't be. I will explain. Kristy, Charlie, Sam, and David Michael are Elizabeth's kids. (She was married once before she married Daddy.) They are my stepsister and stepbrothers. Charlie and Sam are old. They go to high school. David Michael is seven like me, but he does not go to my school. He goes to Margo Pike's school. Emily Michelle is my adopted sister. She is two and a half. Daddy and Elizabeth adopted her from the faraway country of Vietnam. (I named my rat after her.) Nannie is Elizabeth's mother, which makes her my stepgrandmother. She helps take care of the house and all us kids. The pets, too. We have lots of them. Shannon is David Michael's puppy. Boo-Boo is Daddy's fat old cat. And Goldfishie and Crystal Light are (what else?) goldfish. Isn't it lucky Daddy's house is so big?

I made up special nicknames for my brother and me. I call us Andrew Two-Two and Karen Two-Two. (I thought up those names after my teacher read a book to our class. It was called *Jacob Two-Two Meets the Hooded Fang*.) Andrew and I are two-twos because we have two of so many things. We have two houses and two families, two mommies and two daddies, two cats and two dogs. Plus, I have two bicycles, one at each house. (Andrew has two trikes.) And we have clothes and toys and books at each house. This is so we do not have to pack much when we go back and forth.

Here are some other things I have two of:

Glasses — a blue pair for reading, a pink pair for the rest of the time.

Best friends — Hannie Papadakis lives across the street from Daddy and one house down. Nancy Dawes lives next door to Mommy. We call ourselves the Three Musketeers.

Tickly — Tickly is my special blanket. I had to rip Tickly in half so I could have a piece at each house.

Stuffed animals — I have two cats named Moosie and Goosie. They look just the same. Moosie stays at the big house, Goosie stays at the little house.

I think Andrew and I are pretty lucky to be two-twos. Sometimes it is hard, and sometimes we miss the family we are not staying with. But mostly we are very, very lucky. Think how many people love us.

"Kristy?" I said when she answered the phone. "Hi, it is me, Karen."

"Hi, Karen."

Kristy and I had a long talk on the phone. We do that sometimes. Kristy is one of my favorite, favorite people. She told me all about Sea City, New Jersey.

Miss Boss

"Now Emily," I said to my rat. "Remember that you are going on vacation, too. You will be staying with Nancy next door. You know Nancy. And you like her. Nancy will take good care of you." I paused. "I am sorry you cannot come to Sea City with me, but I do not think you would like traveling. You would not like the car ride."

I was getting Emily Junior ready to stay with Nancy. It was Friday afternoon. The next morning we would leave for Sea City. I put Emily's rat supplies into a paper bag.

Then I opened my own suitcase. It was empty. And it smelled funny, sort of musty. But it was not a bad smell. It was just a suit-casey smell. I opened the drawers to my bureau. I began to pull out underwear and shorts and socks. I was looking for my bathing suit when the phone rang. Soon I heard Mommy call, "Karen! For you!"

I ran to the phone. "Hello?" I said.

"Hi. It's me."

Hmm. I wondered who "me" was. "Me" is usually Nancy or Hannie. But this person did not sound like either Nancy or Hannie.

"Hello?" I said again.

"Karen, it's Margo."

"Oh. Hi!"

"Hi. Are you packed yet?"

"I am packing right now."

"I hope you will remember your bathing suit."

"Of course I will remember my bathing suit," I said. I think I sounded a little cross. But for heaven's sake.

"Well, I know you have not been to Sea

City before," said Margo. "And remember a hat. The sun is hot on the beach. Remember sandals, too, for walking around town. Oh, and stamps, in case — "

"Margo," I interrupted her.

" — you want to write any postcards," she finished up.

"Margo," I said again. "I have not been to Sea City before. But I have been to the *beach*. I know what to bring to the beach."

"Okay, okay," said Margo. "I was just trying to help."

You were just being bossy, I thought. Margo Pike was Miss Boss.

I returned to my packing. I did it all by myself. I did not need Miss Boss to help me. She did not know *every*thing.

The next morning I woke up in a flash. I leaped out of bed. It was Sea City Day — and Seth wanted to leave early. "An early start is important," he had said the night before.

As soon as we had eaten breakfast, we

began to load up our car. I had never seen so much stuff — suitcases and blankets and water toys and sheets and towels and some groceries and a box of games and even more. While Seth packed the car, Mommy put Rocky and Midgie into the other car. She was going to drive them to the vet. The vet would board them for two weeks. Nancy was going to take care of Emily Junior and Bob, but she could not care for Rocky and Midgie, too.

"Good-bye!" I called as Mommy drove away.

Later, Nancy ran over. "I am here for the pets," she said importantly.

Andrew and Nancy and I carried Bob and Emily and their things to Nancy's house. Then the three of us ran outside again. Mommy was back. Seth had packed the car. We were ready to leave. And I was excited.

"Good-bye! Good-bye! Good-bye!" Nancy and I called to each other as Mommy pulled out of the driveway. We were on our way to Sea City.

14

Montana and Arizona

There are two things I do not like about long car rides. One is Andrew, the other is Andrew's questions.

Mommy and Seth had decided to divide up the driving. Mommy was going to drive us halfway to Sea City. Seth was going to drive the rest of the way. The trip was going to be lo-o-o-o-ong, since Stoneybrook is in Connecticut and Sea City is in New Jersey. I hoped Andrew would behave.

Guess what. We were still in Stoneybrook when Andrew first said, "How many more

15

minutes until we get there?"

I gave him a Look. "Ten thousand," I told him.

"*Karen,*" said Seth.

"Sorry." I reached into my Fun Bag. Mommy had put together Fun Bags for Andrew and me. Inside them were paper and markers and books and stickers and little toys. "Andrew, look in your Fun Bag," I suggested.

Andrew and I were sitting side by side in the backseat. The Fun Bags were between us. For awhile, we colored quietly. Then I drew some tic-tac-toe boards. Andrew and I played game after game, but I kept winning.

"No fair!" screeched Andrew.

"*Andrew,*" said Seth.

"I know. Let's play the license plate game," I said.

Andrew and I gazed out our windows. We watched the cars go by. I will tell you something. Andrew is not even five yet, and he can already read. I taught him myself. That is how he could play the game.

"New York!" I called out.

"Maine!" Andrew called out.

"Arizona!"

That Arizona car was far from home. So was the one with the Montana license plate. Then Andrew called out, "Hawaii!"

"Andrew, you did not see a car from Hawaii," I said.

"Did too."

"Did not. And quit poking me."

"I am not poking you."

"Yes, you are. Stay on your side of the seat."

Andrew would not stop touching me. Finally I took a roll of Scotch tape out of my Fun Bag. I stuck one end to the middle of the back seat. Then I unrolled it and stuck the other end to the middle of the front seat. "There. That is your side, Andrew. Stay on it."

"I think it is time for a rest stop," said Mommy.

"Probably some old gas station with an

empty candy machine and a smelly bathroom," I said. And Seth gave *me* a Look.

Guess what. I was wrong about the rest stop. It was huge. And it had a Wendy's, a Dunkin' Donuts, not-smelly bathrooms, and a video arcade. First we used the bathrooms. Then we ate a snack at Wendy's. Then we used the bathrooms again. Then Andrew and I played some video games. Then Mommy said we had to use the bathrooms once more. Just to be sure.

Finally we were in the car again, zipping along toward Sea City. We began to see more and more pine trees. The ground began to look sandy. And at last we saw a sign that read SEA CITY — 2 MILES.

"Ooh," I said a few minutes later as we drove along the main street of Sea City. "Look, Andrew. Trampoline Land. Cool!"

"Candy Heaven!" Andrew squealed.

"Crabs for Grabs!"

"Fred's Putt-Putt Course!"

I could already tell we were going to love Sea City.

The Pikes

Seth stopped the car in front of a building. It was not an interesting-looking building. It was the office of the real estate agent. We had to pick up the key to the house we would be renting. When Seth had the key, he climbed back in the car. We drove along until the streets were lined with houses, not stores. Soon Seth turned a corner and drove to the end of the street.

"Hey, I can see the ocean!" I cried.

Sure enough, we had reached the beach.

"And here is our house," said Seth.

It looked just like the house in the photo. Small, but pretty, with a wide front porch. When you step off of the front porch at Mommy's house or at Daddy's house, you step onto grass. Guess what you step onto from the porch at the beach house. Sand. And then you could walk straight to the ocean. I thought that was very cool.

Mommy opened the door to our new home and we looked inside. We saw a living room, a kitchen, and the bedrooms, all on one floor, just as Seth had told me when he showed me the picture. Guess how many bedrooms there were. Three. Perfect. One for Andrew, one for me, and one for Mommy and Seth.

"Can we play in the ocean?" I asked Mommy.

"Not yet," she said. "Unpacking first."

"Boo."

"Karen, you *have* to unpack. You do not even have your bathing suit," pointed out Andrew. "You cannot swim without your suit."

"Oh," I said. "You're right."

Andrew and I helped Seth and Mommy carry things from the car to the house. We made trip after trip. Then Andrew and I decided which bedroom we each wanted. We fought over the one with the bunk beds in it. Seth made us toss a coin for it. Andrew won. Oh, well. Mine was smaller, but it was at the front of the house. When I looked out my window, I looked at the ocean.

"Where is the Pikes' house?" I asked Mommy. She and Seth were putting things away in the kitchen. What I really wanted to ask was, "Can I go swimming yet?" But I knew better.

"Just two houses away, I think," said Mommy.

And at that very moment we heard a knock at our front door. Standing on the porch were all of the Pike kids, plus Jessi Ramsey. These are Margo's brothers and sisters: Mallory, Adam, Byron, Jordan, Vanessa, Nicky, and Claire. Mallory is eleven.

She gets to baby-sit, since she is the oldest. She baby-sits for her brothers and sisters, and she baby-sits for other kids, too. She has even baby-sat for Andrew and me. Adam, Byron, and Jordan are ten years old. They are triplets. And they look exactly alike. Sometimes they are hard to tell apart. Vanessa is nine. She writes poetry. Nicky is eight. He's a pest. And Claire is five, the youngest Pike. Sometimes she and Andrew play together.

Jessi Ramsey is a friend of Mallory's. She baby-sits, too. She and Mallory are even in a club. It is called the Baby-sitters Club, and you can only join it if you are a good baby-sitter. Mal and Jessi are great sitters, and I like them very much. (I like everyone in the club. Kristy is in it, too. In fact, she is the president.) While the Pikes were at the beach, Mal and Jessi were mostly going to be in charge of Mal's brothers and sisters.

"Hi!" Mallory called from the porch.

"Hi!" Mommy replied.

"Jessi and I were just going to take the

kids into town to look around. Would Andrew and Karen like to come with us?"

"Yes, yes, yes!" I cried, jumping up and down.

And Mommy said we could go.

Fun in the Sun

Mallory and Jessi led us down the street, back toward town. Andrew and I looked at the Pikes. Even though Margo was Miss Boss, the bossy bragger, I was glad to have so many kids to play with in Sea City. Andrew can be fun, but he is little, and sometimes he is boring. I decided I could put up with Miss Boss for two weeks. How bad could she be?

We walked down our street and turned left onto a wider street. It was lined with beach houses. Most of them had no lawns, just yards filled with white gravel. Some of the walks were decorated with big seashells. Lots of the houses had decks on top. They looked nice, but I thought, why would you sit on a deck when the beach was so close by, and you could sit on the sand and look at the ocean?

After awhile, the houses became little shops. We had reached the edge of town.

"Welcome to Sea City," said Margo grandly.

I almost said, "We have already driven *through* Sea City," but I did not want to start a fight. Not right away. And not in front of Jessi and Mallory.

Andrew was looking at Margo. "Thank you," he said politely.

Margo smiled at him. "What do you know about Sea City, Andrew?" she asked.

"Not very much," he admitted. "I asked Karen, but she could not tell me anything."

I scowled at my brother. Tattletale.

"Well, I know everything," said Margo.

26

"Margo," Mallory interrupted her sister. "You do not know *every*thing."

"I know almost everything. Now, Andrew, here is one of the most important things about Sea City. Candy Heaven."

"Oh, goody! I was hoping someone would take me here," said Andrew.

We stepped inside. I really did feel as if we were in candy heaven. I had never seen so much penny candy. There was even more than in the candy store in Stoneybrook. (I bought two jaw breakers, one for Andrew and one for me.)

Next we came to a restaurant called Burger Garden.

"This is the coolest place," Margo said. Then she leaned over to me. "Ask Claire what this place is called," she whispered.

"Hey, Claire. What is this place called?" I said.

"Gurber Garden," Claire replied, and everyone laughed.

"Margo? What is a putt-putt course?" Andrew wanted to know. He was reading a sign a block or two away.

"Don't you know?" she replied.

"No, he does not, Miss — " I started to say. "I mean, no he doesn't."

"It is miniature golf," Jessi spoke up.

"Goody!" squeaked Andrew.

"Sea City has Trampoline Land, too," said the bossy bragger.

"Mallory? Can we get ice cream?" asked Nicky.

"Sure," she replied. "Let's go to Ice-Cream Palace."

Miss Boss led the way, of course.

When we left Ice-Cream Palace, we were each holding a cone. (Andrew's was dripping down his hand.) I had chosen a flavor called Fruit Rainbow — even though Margo had said, "That is not the newest flavor, you know."

We walked along with our cones, dripping and slurping and crunching.

"Look at that!" I was pointing to a poster on the front of a store. "Fun in the Sun Festival," I read aloud.

"A festival," said Andrew. "Tell me about it, Margo."

"I — I don't — it must be new," stammered Margo.

At last. Something Miss Boss did not know about.

"*I* will tell you about it," I told Andrew. I turned back to the poster. "The first annual festival," I read aloud. "Food, contests, entertainment, shopping."

"Cool," said Mallory. "I hope we can go."

Boy, so did I.

Sand Castles

The next day was Sunday. When I woke up that morning, the first thing I thought about was Margo. Then I thought about the festival. Then I smiled. Margo had not known anything about the festival, since it was new. She had not known it was going to be held on Friday, the day before we would leave Sea City. She had not known that it would last a whole day. She had not known anything about the contests or the food or the entertainment.

But that had not stopped her from being

a bossy bragger all the way home. I wondered if she would be Miss Boss for the next two weeks. Probably. Oh, well. I was not going to worry about that. I would not let her spoil my vacation.

Sunday was a busy day. Andrew and I ran outside the moment Mommy said we could go. "Stay by the porch!" she called. "Do not go near the water!"

"Okay!" I called back.

As soon as Mommy and Seth had put on their bathing suits, they let us dash across the sand to the waves. Mallory and Jessi and the Pike kids were already on the beach. They had brought along toys and floats and books and flippers and decks of cards. We were ready to play.

"Let's make sand castles!" called Margo when she saw me.

"No, let's go in the water," I said. So we did. We jumped over little waves. We looked for fish. We swam and splashed and shouted.

After awhile, we began to shiver, so we

found our towels and dried off. Then we hunted for shells. (Mostly we found clam shells.) Then the Pike kids wanted to hold races on the beach. At first we just ran regular races. Then we made up new races. Byron invented a towel race. Vanessa invented the slow race — the last person across the finish line was the winner. Guess what. It is hard to move so slowly.

After the slow race (which Nicky won), Margo said, "Okay, Karen, *now* can we make sand castles?"

"Sure," I replied.

"Great. We will have a sand castle-building contest."

"We will?"

"Whoever builds the best castle wins."

"Who will decide which is the best castle?" I wanted to know.

"I will," replied Margo. And that was that.

We set to work on our castles. Margo built a plain old castle. She patted wet sand into the shape of a cone. Then she carved a moat around it.

Big deal.

I made a special dribble castle. I used dribbly wet sand from down by the water to decorate it. When it was finished, my castle looked like a birthday cake with icing dripping down the sides. It was a wonderful fancy castle. I even built a drawbridge over the moat.

Guess what Margo did. She looked at her castle. She looked at my castle. Then she said, "I win!"

I stuck my tongue out at her. I decided not to play with her anymore.

Down the beach I saw Mallory, Adam, Byron, Nicky, Claire, and Andrew playing with some toys I had not seen before. I ran to them. "What are those?" I called.

"Skimboards," replied Byron. He was holding a round, flat board. He tossed it onto the shallowest water he could find, then ran after it, jumped on it, and

skimmed across the water. Behind him, Nicky did the same thing.

"Cool!" I cried. "Can I try?"

"Sure," said Byron. He offered me his board.

"Here, Andrew," said Nicky. "You can try, too." (Andrew shook his head.)

I did what I had seen Byron do — and I fell off the board. I fell four times in all. But soon I was skimming away the rest of the long, sunny day.

I did not play with Margo again.

Karen's Mermaid

On Monday morning, Seth woke up Andrew and me with a surprise. He poked his head first into Andrew's room and then mine, and he said, "Who wants to play miniature golf today?"

"At Fred's Putt-Putt Course?" asked Andrew. "I do!"

"Me too!" I cried.

We spent the morning at Fred's. Andrew and I were not very good players. Andrew even knocked his ball into someone else's game. He got a hole in one, but it did not count, since it had flown through the air and landed in the wrong hole. We had fun anyway, though.

I did not see Margo Pike until after lunch. She was on the beach with her brothers and sisters. They were playing with the skimboards again. Except for Margo. She was lining up her shell collection.

"Hi, Karen! Hi, Andrew!" called Jessi Ramsey. "Want to try the skimboards again?"

I did. Andrew did not. He watched me, though.

After a few rides on the board I ran to Margo. "Did you see me? Did you see how good I was?" I asked. (I was still mad about the sand castle contest. I did not want the bossy bragger to think she was the best at *every*thing.)

"Yup," replied Margo. "You are pretty good. You still fall sometimes, though. I never fall anymore."

"Well, I almost won at miniature golf this morning. And, hey! Look at this shell I

37

found. It is the prettiest of all our shells."

Margo looked over her shell collection. "I have the biggest one," she announced.

"I have the one with the most colors."

"I found a starfish today."

She did? All I had found was a dead blowfish. "Well, Andrew found — " I paused. I looked around for my brother. He was gone, and so was Seth, which was too bad. Andrew had found a piece of driftwood that looked exactly like an owl. "Well, I mean *I* found . . . I mean, I *saw* a — a mermaid. In the ocean."

"Oh, you did not."

"I did too! I saw her this morning. She was swimming out past the waves. . . . She *was*," I insisted, when I saw Margo's face. "She had long, long hair and a bright green scaly fish tail. And she waved to me."

I told Margo such a good story I almost believed it myself.

Neptuna's Visit

Tappety-tappety-tap.

I stirred in my bed. Then I lay still and listened.

Tappety-tappety-tap.

I heard the sound again. I groaned. It could be only one thing. Rain. Rain at my window. "Bullfrogs," I muttered.

It was early Tuesday morning. I was lying in my bed in my room at our beach house. I could not believe it was raining. I wanted to play outside in the sand and the ocean. I did not want to be stuck inside.

Please, please, please, stop raining soon, I thought.

I listened for the *tappety-tappety-tap*. I did not hear it. Had it *already* stopped raining? I leaped out of bed. I pulled up the window shade.

Surprise! The sun was shining brightly, and the sky was clear and blue. It had not been raining at all. I wondered what the tapping noise had been. And that was when I saw it — something outside on the windowsill. I opened the window and pulled the something in.

It was a clam shell. I was sure it had not been there the night before. A folded piece of paper was stuck in it.

I opened the paper, and I found . . . a letter:

Dear Karen,

Hi! It's me, your mermaid. Are you glad to hear from me? I was so happy to find someone who believes in mermaids. I heard you telling Margo about me. People do not see us mermaids

very often, you know. We are hard to see. That is why not many people believe in us.

My name is Neptuna. I live in the ocean in front of your house. I guess I do not have to tell you what I look like, since you have already seen me. I hope you will be staying at your house for a long time. I need a new friend, a friend like you.

I have to ask you a favor right away. The favor is — do not tell any grown-ups about me. Grown-ups are dangerous to mermaids. So can you keep a secret? I hope so. Thank you.

Well, I better go. I need to find something to eat for breakfast. Maybe some tasty seaweed. I will talk to you again soon. 'Bye!

Your New Friend,
Neptuna

I stared at the note. I had never felt so surprised. A mermaid named Neptuna was writing to me? And she wanted me to be her friend? That was so exciting.

And yet . . . hadn't I made up the story

about seeing a mermaid? Hadn't I made it up for Margo?

I thought for a moment. Maybe not. Maybe I thought up the story about the mermaid because I really had seen one, just a little glimpse of one out of the corner of my eye.

Boy, I could hardly wait to tell — I paused. Hmm. Who *could* I tell about Neptuna? Certainly not Mommy or Seth. They were grown-ups. I wondered whether I could tell Hannie and Nancy. They were not grown-ups. On the other hand, Neptuna had asked me to keep her a secret. If I told anyone about her, then I would not be keeping the secret.

I decided I better keep Neptuna a secret from everyone. I would not tell grown-ups or Hannie or Nancy or Andrew or Margo or Mallory or Jessi about her. This was not going to be easy. My big mouth has a little trouble keeping secrets. But Neptuna was worth it.

My very own mermaid.

Neptuna Visits Again

All that day I kept my secret. I did not tell one single person about Neptuna. Also, I did not see her. When I played on the beach, I kept looking out at the ocean. I hoped I would see her head bobbing around, or see her tail flip out of the water. But all I saw were seagulls and fishing boats and a couple of buoys.

"What are you looking for?" Margo asked me once.

"Oh, um, sharks," I replied.

I reminded myself that Neptuna had said mermaids are hard to see.

Four times that day I left the beach and ran to our house. I checked my windowsill for more notes from Neptuna. By dinnertime, none had shown up. After dinner, we went to Ice-Cream Palace for a treat. When we returned, I ran straight to my room and looked out the window.

I found another note! This is what it said:

Hi, Karen!

It is me, Neptuna, again. I know you have been looking for me today. I am sorry I am so hard to see. Mermaids have to be very careful, especially around fishermen and fishing boats. Humans would catch mermaids if they saw us, and we do not want to be caught.

Karen, could you do another favor for me? I need a fork. I have been eating a lot of clams lately. They would be so much easier to eat if I had a fork. But I cannot get one. Just leave it on the sill.

Thank you!

Your New Friend,
Neptuna

A fork. That was easy. Mommy had packed a bag of plastic forks, spoons, and knives for our trip. A plastic fork would probably be okay for clam-eating. I tiptoed into the kitchen and found a clean fork. Then I hurried back to the bedroom with it. I left it out on the sill.

I left a note for Neptuna too:

DEAR NEPTUNA, MY NEW FRIEND,

HERE IS A FORK. I HOPE YOU DO NOT MIND PLASTIC. THANK YOU FOR WRITING TO ME AND BEING MY NEW FRIEND. I CANNOT BELIEVE I KNOW A MERMAID! I AM KEEPING YOUR SECRET. I HAVE NOT TOLD ANY GROWN-UPS.

LOVE, KAREN

* * *

When I woke up the next morning the first thing I did was pull up the window shade. I checked the sill. The fork and the note were gone. I hoped Neptuna was happily eating clams out in the ocean.

On Wednesday, I kept the secret again. And I looked and I looked for Neptuna. But I did not see her.

"*Now* what are you looking for?" Margo asked me.

"Um, pirates," I replied.

I checked my window again that day, but I did not find any notes. I did not really expect to. If Neptuna came out of the water during the day, everyone on the beach would see her. That night I found a note, though. I found it right after Mommy and Seth and Andrew and I came home from the movies. (We saw a fun old movie called *Pollyanna*.)

Yes! Another note! This time Neptuna needed a barrette for her hair. She said her hair was always getting tangled up in sea-weed. And it was floating in front of her eyes. I looked on my dresser. I had an extra barrette. So I set it on the windowsill for my mermaid.

In the morning it was gone.

Karen's Note

"Karen, Karen! Look, I can turn a one-handed cartwheel!"

Margo ran across the sand to me. I was just leaving our house. It was Thursday, and I was ready for another day at the beach.

"A one-handed cartwheel?" I repeated. Hmm. That was pretty good. I could turn a very nice cartwheel — but I needed both hands to do it.

"Sure," replied Margo. "It's cinchy. Watch." Margo put one hand on her hip.

She left it there while she turned a perfect cartwheel. "Ta-dah!" she said when she was finished.

"That was . . . great," I told her.

"You know what else, Karen?" Margo grabbed me by the hand. "Come down to the water. I will show you a trick on the skimboard."

I did not want to see a trick on the skimboard. But I walked to the water with Margo anyway. Most of the Pikes were already there. They were taking turns on the skimboards. As usual, Andrew was watching them. He had not tried the skimboards once.

Margo showed me how she could leap onto a board and skim along one-legged. "Isn't that cool?" she bragged.

I wanted to brag to Margo about something. I *really* wanted to. And I could think of only one thing to brag about. Neptuna. I tried to remember Neptuna's first note. She had said not to tell any *grown-ups* about her. That was all. (Wasn't it?)

I was bursting with my secret.

"Margo," I said suddenly. "I have something amazing to tell you. You are not going to believe this, but it is true. You know that mermaid I saw the other day?"

A funny look crossed Margo's face. "Yeah?" she said.

I moved Margo away from the rest of the Pikes. Then I whispered in her ear, "Well, her name is Neptuna, and we are friends now."

"You are *friends* with a *mer*maid?"

"Yes! Honest." I told Margo about Neptuna's notes, and how she needed a fork for the clams and a barrette for her hair. "In the night she comes and gets the things I leave for her," I added.

"Oh, of *course*."

"She does! She really does. Do you want to see Neptuna's notes? I saved them all. You can see them for yourself."

Margo and I ran to the beach house and I led her to my room. I had hidden Neptuna's notes in a secret pocket in my suitcase. I pulled them out and showed them to her. "There," I said.

The funny look was on Margo's face again. I could tell she was jealous of Neptuna. She wished she had a mermaid of her own.

"Let's go back outside," said Margo.

So we did. The Pike kids were still skimboarding. Andrew was gone, though, and so was Seth. Margo and I decided to bury Mommy in the sand. She was very patient about it. After we had finished, and after we had let Mommy out, I remembered something.

"Margo," I said, "you have to keep Neptuna a secret from grown-ups, okay? If a grown-up saw Neptuna, he would try to catch her. That would be awful. So do not tell." Margo just giggled. "Honest. This is important," I added.

I had to be sure Margo would not tell. I decided that maybe if she saw Neptuna for

herself, she would know just how important the secret was. So that night I left another note for Neptuna. I told her I really,
really needed to be able to see her. Just for
a moment. I asked her how I could do that.

12

"Come to the Light!"

I left my note for Neptuna on the windowsill on Thursday night. On Friday morning when I woke up, I found a note from her. (I wondered why I never heard Neptuna at my window. I decided mermaids must be very quiet creatures.)

Dear Karen,

Thank you for your letter. I will tell you how to call me from the ocean. I will give you a magic mermaid spell. It usually works. But sometimes

I cannot come even when I hear you. If people are nearby or if the tide is too high I will not be able to show up.

Neptuna's note was long. This is what she told me to do: Stand on the rocky jetty in the ocean, wave my arms in circles, and shout out a mermaid-calling chant.

I practiced the chant in my bedroom until I had memorized it. Then I tried waving my arms while I sang, "Mermaid, my mermaid, green and bright, appear from the water. Come to the light!"

I could hardly wait to see Margo that morning. When I did, I ran to her, crying, "Guess what! Guess what!"

Margo looked up from her shell collection. "What?" she said.

"I have mermaid-calling instructions."

Byron was standing next to Margo, and he said, "You mean, like dial 1-800-M-E-R-M-A-I-D?"

"*No*, silly," I replied. I turned back to Margo. "Did you tell your brothers and sisters about Neptuna?" I asked her.

Margo cleared her throat. "Um, yes. I told some of them. You only said not to tell grown-ups."

"Well . . . okay."

"And," Margo went on, "they are dying to see Neptuna."

"Good. Because now I can show her to you."

"Excellent!" Margo jumped to her feet.

"But not right now," I added quickly. "Neptuna said I have to try the chant at exactly twelve o'clock. Noon."

We waited all morning. At five minutes to twelve Margo, Nicky, Claire, Adam, Byron, Jordan, Andrew (I had finally told him about Neptuna), and I met at the jetty. We walked on it in a line to the very end. I faced the ocean. I waved my arms in circles. And I called, "Mermaid, my mermaid, green and bright, appear from the water. Come to the light!"

I stared hard at the ocean. I waited to see circles of little waves, like when a fish jumps out of the water. I was watching for Neptuna's head. I wondered how much of her we would see. Would we see her tail?

We did not see any of her.

I called out the chant again. (Some fishermen on the jetty were staring at me.) I called it out a third time. I waved my arms harder. By now most of the Pikes were snickering. I called the chant *again*.

No Neptuna. She did not appear.

"So where is your mermaid, Karen?" asked Nicky.

"I guess . . . maybe the fishermen scared her," I replied, glancing at them. "Or maybe the tide is too high. I don't know."

I felt very silly. But I knew Neptuna was real, and I wanted the Pikes to see her, especially Margo the bragger. "Maybe I will call her again tomorrow," I told them.

I was not going to stop believing in Neptuna.

Sometime during the night she left another note for me.

13

A Comb for Neptuna

Guess what Neptuna needed this time. A comb for her hair. I decided Neptuna must have very, very long hair, like Ariel's. And I decided it must be hard to take care of, especially underwater. Her note said:

The barrette you gave me helps a lot. But my hair still gets tangled. Do you have a spare comb? I could really use one.

Poor Neptuna. She had no place to buy hair-care products. The only problem was that I *didn't* have a spare comb. I had brought only one to Sea City with me. I could give her mine, but then what would I tell Mommy? I did not want to say I had lost mine. I wanted Mommy to think I was responsible.

I would just have to buy a new comb for Neptuna. And I would have to do it that very day. Neptuna had sounded a bit desperate. Now how was I going to get into town? I was not allowed to go by myself.

Luckily, at breakfast that morning, Mommy said, "Today I need to go to the grocery store and run some other errands. Does anybody want to come with me?"

We all decided to go.

Mommy and Seth and Andrew and I drove into town. Mommy headed for the grocery store.

"Seth?" I said. "Could you take me to the dime store? I just want to look around."

"Sure," replied Seth. "Andrew, do you want to come with us?"

Andrew nodded.

In the dime store, Andrew pulled Seth into the toy aisle. I wandered away. I pretended to be very interested in a Frisbee, in case Seth was watching me. Then I wandered a little further away, into the aisle of socks and underwear. The next thing I knew I was standing by myself in front of a bin of plastic combs. I checked their price. Only 49¢ each. Perfect. In my pocket was a whole dollar.

I paid for a long pink comb while Seth and Andrew were looking at the toys.

"Need a bag?" the clerk asked me.

"Um, no thanks," I said. I stuck the comb and the receipt for it in my pocket.

A few minutes later, my family was standing on the sidewalk in front of the supermarket. Mommy had put the groceries in the car. We were on our way to the fish store when I saw another poster for the Fun in the Sun Festival.

"I cannot wait for the festival," I said. "I wonder what the entertainment will be. Maybe Barney — hey!" I let out a cry.

"What is it?" asked Andrew. "*Is* Barney coming?"

"No. I mean, I don't know. But look, there is going to be a Miss Mermaid Contest." I read from the poster. " 'One lucky young woman will be selected Miss Mermaid. After the contest she will don a mermaid tail, climb into a coach, and bring up the rear of the Fun in the Sun parade.' " This was almost too good to believe. "Oh, my gosh," I said. "I have to enter that contest. I just *have* to be Miss Mermaid."

Mommy leaned closer to the poster. "Karen, I am afraid you cannot enter it," she said. "It isn't for kids. It is for young women who are eighteen to twenty-four years old."

"Boo and bullfrogs," I replied.

"We can still watch the contest," spoke up Seth. "We will go the festival and have some refreshments and then watch the contest and the parade."

Well, that was something. I did wish I could be Miss Mermaid, though.

The Rainy Day

Plinkety-plinkety-plinkety-plink.

When I woke up on Sunday morning it really was raining. I could tell without even getting up. And it was raining hard. So I turned over, snuggled under the blankets, and fell asleep again. The next time I woke up, I padded into the living room. I opened the front door. Mostly what I could see was gray. A low gray sky sending down heavy gray raindrops into a heaving gray ocean. Even the sand and the houses and the life-guards' stand looked gray.

Seth was sitting in an armchair, reading a newspaper.

"Seth?" I said. "Do you think we will have a nice sunny afternoon?"

Seth smiled at me. Then he shook his head. "Not according to the weather report. We are supposed to have rain all day."

"Yuck."

But guess what happened. About an hour later, Jessi and Mallory knocked on our door. "Do you guys want to come over?" Mal asked Andrew and me. She and Jessi shook out their dripping raincoats.

"Could we, Mommy?" I said.

"Of course," she replied.

So Andrew and I spent the entire day at the Pikes' house.

Jessi and Mal are excellent baby-sitters. Almost as good as Kristy. The first thing they said to all us kids, after Andrew and I had taken off our raincoats, was, "Let's put on a play for our parents."

We spent a long time writing our play. We made it up ourselves. It was about ocean creatures whose home is destroyed by a tidal wave, and they have to find a new home. Margo and I fought over who would get to play Daniella, the magic mermaid. Jessi said we could both be mermaids, so we decided to be mermaid twins.

Our play was a hit.

At lunchtime, Mallory said, "Let's have an indoor picnic."

After lunch, Margo said, "Now let's make fudge. I am an expert."

"Well, I am an expert brownie-maker," I said, which was not quite true.

"Well, I am a better expert than you are," replied Margo.

After the fudge we played hide-and-seek, and then Jessi and Mal found board games and card games.

"Come on, Karen. We will play Go Fish," said Margo.

Now I am a very good Go Fish player. That was why I knew Margo was lying when she said no after I said, "Do you have any nines?"

"Liar!" I cried.

"I am not!"

"Are too!"

Margo threw her cards on the floor.

"Margo!" exclaimed her mother. "Apologize to your guest."

"No!"

Mrs. Pike sent Margo to her room. Then I sent myself home. I brought Andrew with me. It had been a long day. We were a little tired. (We remembered to thank the Pikes for the picnic and the fudge and the nice day before we left their house.)

That night I looked at my windowsill before I went to bed, and I found a note! This time Neptuna wrote that she was having some trouble finding enough food in the ocean.

Could you bring me a bag of Murina Mermaid Chow? Any grocery store should have it. I really, really, really need it. Thank you,

Hmm. I had never heard of Murina Mermaid Chow. But if Neptuna needed it that badly, then I would find it for her. I would look for it the very next day.

Mermaid Chow

I did not know how I was going to get into town to buy the Murina Mermaid Chow. I hoped Mommy might say she needed to go to the supermarket again, but she did not. She and Seth and Andrew were ready to spend the day on the beach.

Uh-oh. Neptuna was hungry, and I was supposed to help her. I watched Mommy and Seth gather up towels and sunscreen lotion and books. I wondered what to do. While I was wondering, I heard a knock on the door.

"Hello!" called someone. It was Miss Boss, the card cheater.

"Hi," I said.

"Mal is taking Claire and Nicky and me into town. Want to come, Karen?"

"Oh! Sure!" I cried. This was perfect. What good luck. I guessed my fight with Margo was over. Just in time.

I walked downtown with the Pikes.

"Mal?" said Margo. "Can Nicky and I go to the dime store while you take Claire to the shoe store?" (Claire had lost her sandals.)

"I guess so. But stay right there until I come for you. Karen, what do you want to do?"

"Go to the supermarket," I quickly replied.

Mallory frowned. "The supermarket? Well, okay. Then you stay there, too. Do not leave. Do you understand?"

"Yes." I nodded my head.

But Margo said, "Mallory, can't Nicky and I meet Karen at the grocery store when we are finished? Then we will all wait for you there."

"All right," Mal replied. "But no funny business."

So we split up. I walked into the supermarket by myself. I walked up and down the aisles. In the pet food aisle I found cat chow and dog chow and even some bags of pellets for hamsters and mice and rats and gerbils. But I did not see Murina Mermaid Chow anywhere.

I stepped up to the window of the manager's office. "Excuse me," I said to the woman inside. "Excuse me, but where is the mermaid chow?"

The manager looked puzzled. Then she raised her eyebrows. Finally she began to laugh. "The mermaid chow?" she repeated.

I nodded. "Yes. Murina Mermaid Ch — " I stopped speaking. Behind me I heard more laughter. I turned around. I saw Margo and Nicky. They were covering their mouths with their hands and howling.

Then they took their hands away and laughed even harder.

"What?" I said to them. "What is it?"

"Murina Mermaid Chow?" Margo gasped. "You believed it! You believed everything!" She tried to stop laughing.

"It was all a joke!" Nicky exclaimed. "Neptuna, the notes, everything."

I stepped away from the office. "What do you mean?" I whispered.

"Karen, do you really believe a mermaid swam out of the ocean and dragged herself across the sand every night to leave notes on your windowsill?" asked Margo. (She was still giggling.) "Do you really believe in *mer*maids? Oh — oh, gosh. This is too funny."

"But the notes . . ." I said.

"Vanessa wrote them for us," said Nicky. "We told her what we wanted to say and then she helped us with them. She made up the Murina Mermaid Chow. I did not think you would fall for it. But you did."

MAIL-IN REBATES

MANAGER'S OFFICE

SPECIALS

I could feel my cheeks burning. I had never, ever, ever in my whole entire life been so embarrassed. Margo and Nicky had been making fun of me. They were laughing at me. Even the manager was still laughing at me. I wanted to cry, but I was not going to let Margo and Nicky see that. I clamped my mouth shut. Then I waited for Mallory to arrive.

Karen's Bad Day

I did not say a word as I walked home with the Pikes. Margo and Nicky did not say much either. But they kept laughing and giggling. When Mal asked me if anything was wrong, I just shook my head.

As soon as I could see my house, I ran away from the Pikes. I ran down the street, through the front door, and into my room. Then I flopped on my bed. I lay on my back and stared at the ceiling. I wished Hannie and Nancy were there.

This is what I was thinking: Karen, you

are so stupid. You are a dope. You are a jerk and a twerp and a silly, foolish kindergarten baby. How could you have believed those things? How could you have believed a mermaid was leaving notes on your windowsill? How *could* you?

At lunchtime, Mommy and Seth and Andrew returned to the house.

"Karen? Ready for lunch?" asked Mommy.

"No!" I yelled.

Mommy stuck her head in my room. "Seth is fixing cheese and tomato sandwiches. Don't you want one?"

"No."

Mommy gave me a Look. "Karen, what is the matter?"

"Nothing."

She sat on the edge of my bed. "Are you sure?"

"Yes."

"All right. But I want you to come outside after lunch. You may not mope around all day. Do you understand?"

"Yes."

When lunch was over, I trailed outside after Andrew. The Pikes were on the beach. The boys were playing with the skimboards. Andrew stood and watched them. He stood quietly with his hands behind his back.

"Hey, Andrew!" called Nicky. "Want to try?" (Andrew shook his head.) "You never want to try," said Nicky. "Are you afraid? Are you a scaredy-cat?"

I ran to Andrew's side. "Nicky, you big bully! You shut up! Do you hear me? Andrew is not *afraid*. He just can't ride the skimboard, okay? He is too little. So leave him alone."

Andrew glanced up at me. "Actually," he said quietly, "I can too ride it."

"You can?" I said. I looked at my little brother in surprise. So did the rest of the Pikes.

The Skimboard

The Pike kids and I gathered around Andrew.

"Can you really use the skimboard?" Claire asked him.

"Yup." Andrew nodded.

"Are you *sure*?" I said. "I mean, how do you know?"

Before Andrew could answer me, Nicky handed him the skimboard. "Show us," he said. (He did not sound mean.)

"Okay." Andrew took the board from Nicky. He walked to the edge of the water.

79

(The rest of us followed him.) Then he threw the board, ran after it, leaped on it, and skimmed along until the board came to a gentle stop. Then Andrew stepped off and looked back at us. He did not say, "See? I told you so." But he could have.

The Pike kids and I were staring at Andrew. At first we could not think of a thing to say. Then, finally, Margo let out a breath. "How did you learn how to do that?" she asked.

Andrew had carried the board back to us. He handed it to Nicky. And just then Seth appeared. "Maybe I can help Andrew explain," he said. He put his arm around my little brother.

"You knew he could do this?" I said to Seth.

"Well, I helped him learn," Seth replied. "Andrew wanted to ride the skimboards from the moment he saw them. But he was a little nervous about trying something new in front of so many people."

"I did not want to fall," Andrew spoke up.

"He was afraid someone would laugh at him," added Seth.

"But the first time I tried it, I fell lots of times," I pointed out. "And I still had fun. Even if I do not like being laughed at." I glared at Margo and Nicky then, and they looked down at their feet.

"That's fine, honey," said Seth. "It is good. But you are different from Andrew. Everyone is different. And that is okay. Anyway, I told Andrew I would help him learn how to use a skimboard, but we would do it in private. We bought a board at the dime store, and Andrew has been practicing every day. We walked along the beach to an area that was not so crowded, and Andrew practiced there."

I smiled at my shy brother. "And that is how you got so good," I said.

"Am I really that good?" asked Andrew.

"Good?" exclaimed Margo. "You are practically an expert!"

"Hey does this mean we have our own skimboard?" I asked Seth.

"Yup," he replied. "You can go get it. It's on the porch, hidden behind the deck chair."

I dashed across the sand to our house, found the board, and brought it back to the beach. "Come on!" I cried. "We can have races!"

"Cool!" said Margo.

But I turned to her fiercely. "Not you," I said. "And not Nicky. Maybe not Vanessa, either. You are the meanest people I know. You cannot be in any race I am in. Also," I went on, "after right now, I am not speaking to you, and I am not playing with you for the rest of the vacation. And maybe not ever again."

"But — " Margo started to say. She looked as if she might cry.

I turned my back on her anyway. "Okay.

Let the skimboard races begin. Andrew, come here. You, too, Claire. And Adam, Byron, and Jordan, but nobody else. Nobody else is allowed."

We played on the skimboards for a long time. Andrew had fun with us. Once, he even beat Byron in a race. I kept my word, though. I did not let the meanies play with us. They had to play by themselves.

Festival Day

I could not believe that my beach vacation was almost over.

It was Friday. This was bad and good. It was bad because the very next day we would have to pack up our car and leave Sea City. It was good because it was . . . festival day! Very soon, Mommy and Seth and Andrew and I were going to walk into town for the Fun in the Sun Festival.

"Karen?" said Andrew. "Are you going to ask Margo to come with us?"

"*No,*" I answered. "I mean, no, Andrew. She is going with her family."

"Are you still mad at Margo?"

"Yes."

"Nicky too?"

"Yes."

"But why?"

"Because they are meanie-meanie-mos. They did something that was not very nice, and they did not even say they were sorry."

"Oh."

I hoped Andrew would forget about Margo for awhile. *I* wanted to forget about her, at least for the day. I wanted to enjoy the festival. I did not want to talk about Margo all the time.

When Mommy and Seth and Andrew and I walked downtown, we found that Sea City was very crowded. People were everywhere. The stores had opened their doors, and the storekeepers had set up stands on the sidewalks. In the streets, vendors walked back and forth calling, "Candy apples! Get your candy apples here!" or "Italian ices!" or "Soft drinks and pretzels!" or "Salt water taffy! Our specialty!" At other stands you could buy hamburgers and hot-dogs, fried clams, popcorn shrimp, fish sandwiches, seafood salads, and crab cakes. Another stand sold nothing but desserts. I had never seen so much food.

Andrew was all set to eat lunch (he said he wanted to try clams), when, at the same time, he and I saw . . . a Ferris wheel, a merry-go-round, a funhouse, a whiplash, and midway games where you could win prizes.

"Look! A carnival!" I exclaimed.

Oh, boy. So much to see and do. Near the carnival was a banner advertising a Battle of the Bands. Local bands were playing in a tent, competing for a trophy that would say FIRST PLACE — FUN IN THE SUN BATTLE OF THE BANDS. I could hear loud music, and a woman singing into a microphone.

We could not decide what to do first.

Andrew said, "Let's go on the rides!"

I said, "Let's try to win some prizes."

Mommy said, "How about lunch?"

And Seth said, "Who wants to listen to the battle of the bands?"

In the end, we did everything. Later in the afternoon we were walking down the street with sticky ice-cream cones and little stuffed animals and some souvenirs, when I noticed a stage in front of a tent. Walking across the stage was a line of young women wearing fancy dresses.

"The Miss Mermaid contest!" I cried. I had almost forgotten about it. "Can we watch for awhile?" I asked.

Mommy and Seth said yes, so we squirmed our way to the front of the crowd, right next to the stage. An announcer stood at the end of the stage. He was saying, "As soon as our Miss Mermaid has been selected, she will put on her mermaid costume and her crown, and ride through town in her coach in our wonderful Fun in the Sun parade. And now I am pleased to announce that our very first Miss Mermaid is . . ."

At that moment I felt someone bump my elbow. I looked around to find that I was standing right next to my enemy, Margo Pike.

Miss Mermaid

Margo and I glared at each other. Then I turned my head away. I looked back at the announcer. He was saying, " . . . our very first Miss Mermaid is Belinda Scott. Congratulations!"

The crowd cheered and clapped for Belinda Scott.

But not me. I looked back at Margo. I said, "What are *you* doing here?"

"I am watching the Miss Mermaid contest," Margo replied primly.

"Well, go somewhere else."

"*You* go somewhere else."

"I would if I could move," I said. But I could not move. It was too crowded. People were to my left, to my right, and behind me. In front of me was the stage. I was trapped.

"Attention! Attention, please! Quiet down," said the announcer. "If everyone will please look over there (he pointed across the crowd), "you will see Miss Mermaid's coach."

I turned and saw a coach that looked like Cinderella's — round and pink, sparkling and glittering. "Ooh," I said softly.

"In just a moment," the announcer went on, "I will escort Miss Mermaid to her coach so that she may ride in the parade, which is about to begin. However, Miss Mermaid must do one important thing first. She is going to pick two lucky girls from the crowd to ride with her as little mermaids. Miss Mermaid, who do you choose?"

Belinda Scott looked out at the crowd. Then she looked down. She looked straight at Margo and me. "I choose these two girls," she said.

Me? Miss Mermaid had chosen *me*? I was going to get to ride in the coach? I let out a shriek. I could not believe it. "Yea!" I cried. "Oh, thank — " I stopped. Miss Mermaid had also chosen Margo. I was going to have to ride with my enemy.

I looked at Margo. She was glaring at me. We stuck our tongues out at each other. "Bossy bragger meanie-mo," I hissed.

The next thing I knew, I was waving good-bye to Mommy and Seth. Someone was helping Margo and me slip into mermaid costumes, while Miss Mermaid put on her own costume. And her crown, of course. Then someone else helped us into the coach. Ahead of us, the parade had begun. We were going to bring up the rear.

"Be sure to wave," Miss Mermaid said to

Margo and me. "And smile. Smile at every-one." She paused. "You two look adora-ble," she added. "Are you sisters? Or best friends?"

We did not have a chance to answer. Our coach began to move then. Miss Mermaid stopped looking at Margo and me. She looked at the crowd instead.

I turned to Margo. "Bossy bragger meanie-mo," I whispered again.

"Baby, baby, baby," Margo whispered back. "Why did you lie to me?"

"I did not lie!"

"Yes, you did. About seeing a mermaid."

"Well, you cheated."

"I did not!"

Margo and I were whispering as loudly as we could. We were trying to smile at the crowd at the same time.

"You and Nicky *laughed* at me!" I whispered.

"What?" Margo could not hear me. Then she said something else.

"What?" I replied.

Margo started to smile. "We are having a whisper fight," she said.

I did not want to smile, but I couldn't help it. "I guess we are." That was a very silly idea. Margo and I grinned at each other.

Home Again

I did not think Margo would ever be one of my best friends, like Nancy or Hannie. I did not think she would ever be one of my very good friends. But I knew we were regular friends again. Our whisper fight had shown me that. If we could laugh about what had happened, we were probably not angry about it anymore.

When the parade was over and our coach had come to a stop, someone helped Miss Mermaid and Margo and me onto the sidewalk. Then we changed out of our mermaid tails and into our clothes. Mommy was waiting for me. Mrs. Pike was waiting for Margo. The four of us walked home together.

"You know what?" I said to Mommy as we stepped onto our porch. "This is our last night in Sea City. And we will eat our last dinner here. Everything that happens from now on will be the *last*. We will go to bed in our beach-house beds for the last time, we will wake up in them tomorrow morning for the last time, we will eat breakfast in our kitchen here for the last time, we will have one last swim in the ocean — "

"Karen," Mommy interrupted me. "How about eating at Burger Garden tonight for the last time?"

"Yes!" I cried.

And that is what we did. Afterward, we walked home along the beach, instead of the streets. Andrew saw a falling star. Then we sat on our porch and played Old Maid. And *then* Mommy and Seth said they wanted to do a little packing. I played one more game of Old Maid with my brother before we went to bed. (He beat me.)

The next morning I woke up early. Before we left Sea City, I wanted to build a sand castle, swim in the ocean, find seashells for Hannie and Nancy, and stand on the jetty watching the fishermen.

I had time to do most of those things before Seth said, "Okay, kids. Time to load up the car. Change out of your bathing suits, please."

Boo. Our vacation was over.

An hour later my family and I were driving through Sea City. As we passed Ice-Cream Palace, Andrew said, "How many more minutes until we get there?"

Since he looked as if he really wanted to know, I tried to figure it out. "About two hundred or maybe two hundred and fifty," I guessed.

"Two hundred *minutes*?" Andrew looked shocked.

"Get out your Fun Bag," I suggested.

Andrew and I both pulled out our Fun Bags. Soon we were playing games and drawing pictures. Not long after that, we were fighting.

"Andrew is on my side again!" I squawked. "He crossed the line!"

Mommy said it was time for a rest stop.

After the rest stop, Andrew and I fell asleep. When we woke up, we were pulling into our driveway in Stoneybrook. Nancy and Hannie were sitting on our front porch. Emily Junior's cage and Bob's cage were between them.

"Welcome home!" they cried.

I woke up fast. I leaped out of the car. "Hi! Hi, we are back!" I exclaimed. "I brought you seashells! How have you been? How is Emily Junior? Did she behave herself?"

"She was fine," said Nancy. "How was Sea City?"

"It was excellent! I got to ride in a parade and we built sand castles, and Andrew and I learned to ride skimboards. Oh, but

Margo and I had a *huge* fight. She played a trick on me."

"Meanie-mo," said Nancy and Hannie at the same time. (My best friends and I always stick up for each other. That is why we are the Three Musketeers.)

"Do you want me to tell you what she did?" I asked. "It all started with a mermaid story." Hannie and Nancy and I took Emily upstairs to my room. Then I began to tell them the story of Neptuna, my mermaid.

About the Author

ANN M. MARTIN lives in New York City and loves animals, especially cats. She has two cats of her own, Mouse and Rosie.

Other books by Ann M. Martin that you might enjoy are *Stage Fright*; *Me and Katie (the Pest)*; and the books in *The Baby-sitters Club* series.

Ann likes ice cream and *I Love Lucy*. And she has her own little sister, whose name is Jane.

Little Sister

Don't miss #53

KAREN'S SCHOOL BUS

It was Monday. Bus day!

I put on my favorite outfit in honor of my first school bus ride. This is what I wore: black leggings, yellow socks, black sneakers, yellow taxi cab sweater. (I would have worn a school bus sweater. But I did not have one. I hoped this would not hurt the bus driver's feelings.)

The bus stop was just down the street. I walked there by myself. Hannie and her brother, Linny, were waiting with a few other kids from our block. Linny is David Michael's friend.

"Hi, everyone!" I called.

I was gigundoly excited about my first school bus morning.

Little Sister

by Ann M. Martin
author of The Baby-sitters Club®

More Titles... ➡

❏ MQ48231-9	#59	Karen's Leprechaun	$2.95
❏ MQ48305-6	#60	Karen's Pony	$2.95
❏ MQ48306-4	#61	Karen's Tattletale	$2.95
❏ MQ48307-2	#62	Karen's New Bike	$2.95
❏ MQ25996-2	#63	Karen's Movie	$2.95
❏ MQ25997-0	#64	Karen's Lemonade Stand	$2.95
❏ MQ25998-9	#65	Karen's Toys	$2.95
❏ MQ26279-3	#66	Karen's Monsters	$2.95
❏ MQ26024-3	#67	Karen's Turkey Day	$2.95
❏ MQ26025-1	#68	Karen's Angel	$2.95
❏ MQ26193-2	#69	Karen's Big Sister	$2.95
❏ MQ26280-7	#70	Karen's Grandad	$2.95
❏ MQ26194-0	#71	Karen's Island Adventure	$2.95
❏ MQ26195-9	#72	Karen's New Puppy	$2.95
❏ MQ26301-3	#73	Karen's Dinosaur	$2.95
❏ MQ26214-9	#74	Karen's Softball Mystery	$2.95
❏ MQ69183-X	#75	Karen's County Fair	$2.95
❏ MQ69184-8	#76	Karen's Magic Garden	$2.95
❏ MQ69185-6	#77	Karen's School Surprise	$2.99
❏ MQ69186-4	#78	Karen's Half Birthday	$2.99
❏ MQ69187-2	#79	Karen's Big Fight	$2.99
❏ MQ69188-0	#80	Karen's Christmas Tree	$2.99
❏ MQ69189-9	#81	Karen's Accident	$2.99
❏ MQ69190-2	#82	Karen's Secret Valentine	$3.50
❏ MQ69191-0	#83	Karen's Bunny	$3.50
❏ MQ69192-9	#84	Karen's Big Job	$3.50
❏ MQ69193-7	#85	Karen's Treasure	$3.50
❏ MQ69194-5	#86	Karen's Telephone Trouble	$3.50
❏ MQ06585-8	#87	Karen's Pony Camp	$3.50
❏ MQ06586-6	#88	Karen's Puppet Show	$3.50
❏ MQ06587-4	#89	Karen's Unicorn	$3.50
❏ MQ06588-2	#90	Karen's Haunted House	$3.50
❏ MQ55407-7		BSLS Jump Rope Pack	$5.99
❏ MQ73914-X		BSLS Playground Games Pack	$5.99
❏ MQ89735-7		BSLS Photo Scrapbook Book and Camera Pack	$9.99
❏ MQ47677-7		BSLS School Scrapbook	$2.95
❏ MQ43647-3		Karen's Wish Super Special #1	$3.25
❏ MQ44834-X		Karen's Plane Trip Super Special #2	$3.25
❏ MQ44827-7		Karen's Mystery Super Special #3	$3.25
❏ MQ45644-X		Karen, Hannie, and Nancy	
		The Three Musketeers Super Special #4	$2.95
❏ MQ45649-0		Karen's Baby Super Special #5	$3.50
❏ MQ46911-8		Karen's Campout Super Special #6	$3.25

Available wherever you buy books, or use this order form.

Scholastic Inc., P.O. Box 7502, Jefferson City, MO 65102

Please send me the books I have checked above. I am enclosing $_____
(please add $2.00 to cover shipping and handling). Send check or money order – no
cash or C.O.Ds please.

Name_____Birthdate_____

Address_____

City_____State/Zip_____

Please allow four to six weeks for delivery. Offer good in U.S.A. only. Sorry, mail orders are not
available to residents to Canada. Prices subject to change.   BSLS497